SEVEN OF WANDS

A SHORT RIVALS TO LOVERS, AGE GAP, TAROT ROMANCE

TAROT FANTASIES

JAX WILDER

Published by Rainbow Quartz Publishing

RQPublishing.com

RainbowQuartzPublishing@gmail.com

Edmonds, WA 98026

ISBN: 978-1-961714-63-2

Cover design by Miranda Townsend

Edited by Miranda Townsed

First Edition: December 2024

You deserve to be loved too.

CHAPTER ONE

I pushed open the creaky door of the Arcane Room, the scent of incense hitting me immediately. Shelves lined with candles, crystals, and odd trinkets filled the cozy space. My daughter swore by this place—said it helped with her stress and the occasional *bad juju*. I wasn't so sure, but I wasn't one to argue with her about it.

Ms. Vesper greeted me with a warm smile from behind the counter. "Layla, darling, I've got that candle your daughter set aside for you."

"Perfect," I said, making my way to the counter. "She said I needed it to clear out all the negativity from the divorce and all."

Ms. Vesper chuckled, shaking her head. "That's what she mentioned. I've always loved your daughter's energy. She's a regular here."

"Yeah, she's always been into this stuff. Me? Not so much, but... here I am."

Ms. Vesper placed the candle into a small box and tied it with a piece of twine. As she handed it to me, she looked up, her gaze softening. "Your daughter also mentioned how disappointed you were about missing the National Bowling Championships this year."

I sighed. "Yeah, well, there's always next year. It's been a rough one, you know?"

She nodded, but the way she looked at me said she wasn't buying my nonchalance. "Are you taking care of yourself, Layla?"

"Of course," I lied.

Her brow shot up, eyes narrowing in disbelief. "Really?"

I hesitated, feeling like a kid caught sneaking cookies before dinner. "I'm... getting by."

"Hmm," she hummed, crossing her arms. "Do you have twenty minutes?"

I glanced at my watch, unsure where this was going. "I guess..."

"Good. Come with me. Draw a card."

I blinked. "A tarot card?"

"Trust me. You might find it interesting." She led me over to a small wooden table with a deck of tarot cards neatly stacked in the center. "Go ahead," she urged. "Pick one."

I reached out hesitantly and pulled a card from

the middle of the deck. The Seven of Wands stared back at me.

Ms. Vesper smiled knowingly. "The Seven of Wands is about perseverance, standing your ground, and facing challenges head-on. It tells me you've been fighting hard, Layla."

I chuckled softly. "Yeah, well... that's one way to put it."

She stood, giving me a long look. "Now, follow me." I followed her through the narrow hallway to a small white room with a black chase lounge. "Sit here. I'll be right back."

When she returned, she handed me a steaming cup of tea. "Drink this," she said gently. "And remember to enjoy yourself."

Before I could ask her what that even meant, I took a cautious sip of the tea. It had a strange, almost floral taste. A moment later, the room spun, and I blinked hard.

When I opened my eyes, I wasn't in the Arcane Room anymore.

The sound of a slot machine chimed in the distance. I was standing in a grand hotel lobby, surrounded by marble floors and glittering chandeliers. A large fountain gurgled in the center of the room. My breath hitched.

This was Vegas.

How the hell did I get to Vegas?

I took a few steps forward, the covers over my

bowling shoes squeaking against the polished floor. Bowling shoes. Right. I looked down. I was still in my bowling shirt and jeans. I made my way to the front desk, the surreal nature of my situation still sinking in.

As I reached the counter, a man turned away from the clerk, bumping into me. He was tall, broad-shouldered, with dark hair and an annoyingly attractive smirk.

"Oh, sorry about that," he said, flashing a smile that was entirely too charming for my peace of mind.

"Uh, no problem," I muttered, stepping aside to let him pass. Our eyes met for a brief moment, and something sparked—like a flicker of recognition, though I was sure I'd never seen him before. He gave me one last smile and walked off.

"Next," the clerk called.

I blinked, still feeling off-kilter from the collision, but stepped forward. "Where am I?"

"Ms. Price, right?" the clerk asked without hesitation.

My brows furrowed. How did she know my name? "Uh, yeah..."

"You're in room 912, South Wing. Did you need another key?"

"Um... yes, thank you." I hesitated, glancing back at the guy who had bumped into me, but he was already disappearing around the corner.

I took the key from the clerk and tried to shake off the weirdness. The Arcane Room was always strange, but this? This was next level. I decided to roll with it. Maybe this was part of the challenge Ms. Vesper had mentioned.

I made my way up to my room, still in a bit of a daze. The elevator ride felt endless, and when I finally reached the ninth floor, I found myself standing in front of the door marked *912*. A shiny gold plaque beside the door read *The President's Suite*.

I opened the door, and my jaw dropped. The suite was massive. The kind of luxury I'd only seen in magazines. Floor-to-ceiling windows framed the sparkling Vegas skyline, and a plush couch sat in the middle of the room, all sleek and modern.

I wandered through in a daze, pushing open double doors that led to a bedroom the size of my entire house. A California king bed sat in the center, the comforter so fluffy it looked like a cloud. I couldn't resist. I walked over and let myself fall backward onto the bed, sinking into it perfectly.

A bottle of champagne sat on the side table, alongside a welcome basket. I picked up the card that rested beside it.

Welcome to the National Bowling Competition.

I stared at the card. Was this really happening? Was I really here to bowl?

I shuffled through the rest of the papers and

found a schedule of events and a list of my bowling times. This was my dream.

I shook my head, the disbelief lingering. How did I end up here? And what about my bowling ball?

I glanced over at the closet and, sure enough, there they were. Two gleaming bowling balls, freshly polished, along with several outfits hanging neatly on the rack.

I smiled to myself. Maybe this was exactly what I needed after all.

CHAPTER TWO

After sinking into the massive bed and letting the luxury of it wash over me, I decided I'd had enough lounging for one morning. The first event wasn't for a little while, but curiosity got the better of me. I needed to stretch my legs and get a feel for where everything was—especially the bowling alley.

Vegas, of course, was exactly how I remembered it from my younger days. Loud, bright, full of life. But I wasn't the thrill-seeker I once pretended to be. Gambling never held much appeal for me; I preferred more tangible ways to spend my money. Trips, good food, things that made memories. Not risking it all on the pull of a slot machine. Still, there was something about the energy in the air that made my skin tingle. Maybe it was the flash of lights or the never-ending buzz of chatter and excitement all around me, but I couldn't help but feel a small thrill as I stepped out of the elevator.

The hotel was massive—one of those sprawling Vegas resorts that seemed like a city unto itself. After wandering past endless rows of slot machines and blinking lights, I finally found the bowling area. Large banners announced the *National Mixed Bowling Championship*, the bright colors pulling me toward the entrance.

Bowling had always been my one escape, even back when life was simpler. Before the kids, before the divorce, and before I forgot how to take time for myself. Maybe that's why I was here, standing in the middle of Las Vegas, holding a key to a suite I could never have afforded on my own.

I made my way to the registration desk, where a long line of competitors and teams stood chatting, laughing, and exchanging knowing glances. This was it—the energy, the anticipation I missed. The competitive edge that kept me coming back to bowling year after year. Even if this year had nearly passed me by.

"Here to sign in?" the woman at the desk asked, glancing up from her clipboard.

"Yeah," I replied, handing her my registration info. "Layla Price."

She flipped through some papers, nodded, and handed me a small packet. "You're all set, Ms. Price. Welcome to the competition."

I took the packet and thanked her, stepping aside to glance through the information. It contained my match times, lanes, and some general rules about the tournament. I smiled to myself. It was really happening.

"Fancy seeing you here."

The voice was familiar, and when I looked up, there he was. The man from the front desk earlier, with that same cocky smile and a relaxed confidence that radiate off him. He leaned against the wall, arms crossed, looking far too comfortable for someone about to face some serious competition.

"You again," I said, raising an eyebrow. "Do you make a habit of sneaking up on people?"

He grinned, the kind that made you want to either slap him or kiss him. "Only on women who look like they could use a bit of competition."

"Competition?" I narrowed my eyes at him. "I hope you're not implying what I think you are."

"Well," he said, pushing off the wall and stepping closer, "you do look like a serious contender. But you know, not everyone can handle the pressure."

There was something about his tone—a teasing edge—that lit a fire inside me. It wasn't just his words, though. It was the way he carried himself, like he knew exactly how to push buttons and get under my skin.

"Don't worry," I said, smiling sweetly, "I don't plan on cracking under any pressure."

He tilted his head, amusement flickering in his eyes. "Good. Because I'd hate to see you lose before you even start."

I folded my arms, stepping forward so that there was barely an inch between us. "I'll have you know, I've been bowling longer than you've probably been alive."

He chuckled, a low sound that sent a shiver down my spine. "I wouldn't be so sure about that. But I do appreciate the confidence."

"Confidence?" I shot back. "I call it skill."

He nodded, clearly enjoying this little back-and-forth. "We'll see about that. Hope you're ready for some real competition."

"Trust me," I said, stepping back and giving him a once-over, "I'm always ready."

Before he could respond, one of the tournament officials called out, motioning for everyone to gather for a quick briefing. I glanced back at the guy, giving him a nod before heading over to join the group.

But as I walked away, I couldn't help the small smile tugging at the corners of my lips. There was something about him—about this moment—that made me feel alive again. A thrill I hadn't felt in years.

As the official went through the logistics of the event, I found my mind drifting back to Drake. I hadn't flirted with anyone in years—not since my ex, and certainly not with the kind of energy that I'd felt just now. And yet, here I was, practically sparring with this guy, feeling that same rush I used to get when life was simpler. It was... unexpected. I wasn't about to let him distract me though.

Not yet, anyway.

When the briefing wrapped up, I headed over to the lanes to get a feel for the space. It wasn't like my usual alley back home—this place was huge, filled with professional-grade lanes and the kind of fancy technology, and string pins, not to mention the sheer size. There are sixteen lanes at home—there are ninety here. This wasn't just a casual game; this was the real deal.

I scanned the room, watching as teams practiced and prepared, the air was laced with competition and excitement. My nerves buzzed, but it wasn't just from the tournament. It was from *him*—the way he seemed to settle into my thoughts, as if daring me to let down my guard.

And then, as if on cue, the tall dark haired muscular thirty something appeared beside me again, leaning casually against the ball return.

"Not bad, huh?" he asked, glancing around. "I'm Drake."

I raised an eyebrow. "You here to talk or to bowl?"

He grinned. "Why can't it be both?"

"Because I don't mix business with pleasure."

"Ah," he said, leaning in slightly. "So, you admit there's potential for pleasure?"

I opened my mouth to respond, but the words caught in my throat. He was good—too good. Before I could come up with a witty comeback, he stepped back, grabbed his bowling ball and gave me a quick nod.

"See you on the lanes, Layla. Try not to lose your focus."

I watched him walk away, feeling that familiar rush of excitement and, if I was honest with myself, something else. Something I hadn't felt in a long time.

I wasn't here to flirt or get distracted. I was here to bowl. But still... it didn't hurt to have a little fun along the way.

CHAPTER THREE

I stood at the end of the lane, the weight of the ball comforting in my hand. The smooth texture beneath my fingers was familiar, grounding me in a way that little else had since my life started unraveling. The noise of the alley—laughter, pins crashing, the murmur of conversations—was muted as I focused on the lane ahead. All that mattered in this moment was my next shot.

Across from me, Drake leaned casually against the ball return, a smug grin on his face. He had a confidence that was impossible to ignore, the kind that wasn't born from arrogance but from knowing you were damn good at what you did. He watched me, eyes glinting with amusement, as if he knew something I didn't.

I took a deep breath, lining up my shot. My fingers slipped into the holes of the ball, my body falling into rhythm. This was my game. I'd been bowling for decades. There wasn't a single thing he could say to throw me off.

"Not bad form," he called out, his voice playful but laced with challenge. "But you might want to scoot over—half a board."

I froze mid-motion, glancing at him over my shoulder. "Excuse me?"

"You're off-center by half a board," he said with a shrug. "Just saying. But hey, you do you. I just prefer to win against the best."

I narrowed my eyes at him. I knew my approach, knew my stance. But something about the way he said it, the casual confidence in his voice, made me second-guess myself.

"I'm fine where I am," I shot back.

"Sure," he said, crossing his arms, "but wouldn't you rather crush me at my best?"

I hated that he was getting in my head, but even more, I hated that he was probably right. With a resigned sigh, I stepped half a board over, glaring at him as I did it.

"Better?" I asked.

"Let's see," he replied, raising an eyebrow.

I focused back on the lane, re-centering myself. The moment stretched as I took my steps, the ball leaving my fingers with a satisfying roll. It barreled down the lane, dead-center, and slammed into the pins with a satisfying crack. Strike.

I turned slowly to find Drake watching me, the corner of his mouth twitching as if he were trying not to smile.

"Not bad," he said, finally letting the grin break free. "Guess my advice worked."

"Please," I said, walking back toward him, my heart still racing from the shot. "That was all me."

"Right," he said with a wink. "But if you ever want to thank me, I'll be around."

I couldn't help but smile despite myself. There was something thrilling about this banter, the playful back-and-forth. It had been years since anyone had flirted with me like this—so openly, so effortlessly.

As Drake stepped up to take his turn, I found myself watching him. He had the kind of ease about him that came from years of practice, and yet every movement was precise, calculated. He lined up his shot, his focus sharp, and with a swift movement, sent the ball down the lane.

Strike.

He turned, catching my eye, the smirk back in full force. "Told you, I prefer to play against the best."

"Don't get cocky," I replied, though the thrill of competition was buzzing in my veins.

The game continued, strike after strike, spare after spare, each of us refusing to give an inch. The tension between us was electric, crackling with every turn. But it wasn't just the competition—it was something more, something unspoken that hung in the air between us.

As I set up for what would be my final shot, I could feel Drake's eyes on me, watching, waiting. It was close—too close. I could win with this strike, but if I missed... well, let's just say I wasn't planning on missing.

I took a deep breath, lined up my shot, and released. The ball sped down the lane, curving slightly at the last moment before smashing into the pins. Strike.

A grin spread across my face as I turned to face him.

"Looks like I win," I said, a little breathless from the adrenaline.

Drake walked up, shaking his head in mock defeat. "Alright, I'll give you that one. But don't get too comfortable. We've got more games ahead."

I felt a surge of satisfaction, a feeling I hadn't experienced in so long—the thrill of being in control, of winning. But more than that, it was the spark between us, the way he looked at me, like I wasn't just some woman going through the motions but someone worth competing against. Worth flirting with.

"You're not going to let me enjoy this, are you?" I teased.

"Not a chance," he replied, his smile widening. "I prefer a challenge."

"Well," I said, stepping closer to him, "get ready, because I'm just getting started."

His eyes darkened slightly, the playful banter giving way to something more intense for just a moment. Then, with a wink, he stepped back and nodded toward the lanes.

"Game on, Layla."

CHAPTER FOUR

The second game kicked off with a different energy. Gone was the initial awkwardness of figuring out where we stood—now it was pure competition, but with something more simmering beneath the surface. Something I hadn't felt in years.

Drake and I moved around each other like we were playing a different kind of game, one where the stakes weren't just points on a scoreboard. There was a charge in the air that had nothing to do with bowling and everything to do with the way his eyes lingered on me just a second too long or the way my skin seemed to tingle whenever he came near.

I picked up my ball, feeling the familiar weight in my hand, but my focus wasn't just on the pins anymore. Every time Drake moved closer, every time he brushed past me, there was this... awareness. It was like the air between us had thickened with something unspoken but undeniably there.

I stepped onto the lane, lining up my shot. As I prepared to throw, Drake's voice drifted over from behind me.

"You look a little tense, Layla. Sure you don't need a warm-up first?"

I smirked, not looking back. "I'm good, thanks."

He chuckled softly, and I could practically feel his eyes on me as I released the ball. It rolled down the lane, curving and crashing into the pins, sending them scattering. Nine pins. Not bad, but not perfect.

"Nice," he said, stepping closer as I walked back toward him. "Almost had it."

I could hear the teasing in his voice, but when he brushed past me to take his turn, his arm grazed mine just lightly enough to send a jolt through me. It wasn't just a touch—it was deliberate. He knew exactly what he was doing, and I hated how much I loved it.

I watched him step up to the lane, his movements fluid, confident. There was something about the way he carried himself that drew me in—like he knew exactly how to get under my skin. And judging by the sly smile that played on his lips as he released his ball and knocked down all ten pins with ease, he knew it too.

He turned, that cocky grin back in place. "Strike. Told you I prefer to win."

I rolled my eyes, but the truth was, I didn't mind the teasing. In fact, I was starting to crave it. There was something about the way he pushed me, the way we bickered and flirted that made my pulse race in ways it hadn't in a long time.

"You get one strike, and suddenly you're king of the lanes?" I said, grabbing my ball for the next frame.

He shrugged, his eyes sparkling with mischief. "I just call it like I see it."

I stepped up again, trying to shake the distraction he had become. But it wasn't easy. Every time I moved, I was hyper-aware of his presence. The heat of his gaze followed me as I lined up my shot, making my skin prickle with a mixture of nerves and something else—something that made my heart race.

I sent the ball down the lane, but my focus was off. The ball veered to the left, and I cursed under my breath as it missed the pins entirely.

"Gutter ball, huh?" Drake's voice was laced with amusement as he stepped beside me, close enough that our arms brushed again. This time, the contact lingered.

I shot him a look. "Don't get too comfortable. The game's not over yet."

"Oh, I'm very comfortable," he replied, his voice dropping just slightly, making the words sound more like a promise than a tease.

My breath caught in my throat. He wasn't just flirting—he was making it clear that this was about more than the game. And the way his hand hovered just a fraction of an inch from mine, as if he was resisting the urge to touch me again, made my pulse race.

The rest of the game passed in a blur of strikes, spares, and near misses, but the tension between us only grew. Every time he moved, every glance he sent my way, every playful jab he made, it felt like another layer of anticipation was added to the mix.

And it wasn't just his words. I started noticing the little things—how he watched me with that slow, deliberate gaze whenever I lined up my shots, how his lips would curve just slightly when he won a frame, how he always seemed to stand just close enough that our shoulders or arms would brush when we passed each other.

I hated how much I was noticing, how much I wanted him to touch me, to press against me just a little more. But at the same time, I loved it. I hadn't felt this kind of pull, this electric charge, in years—not since long before the divorce, when life settled into a monotonous routine. Now, here I was, in the middle of Las Vegas, feeling more alive than I had in a long, long time.

The game came down to the last few frames, both of us neck and neck. But Drake, damn him, managed to pull off three perfect strikes in the final round, leaving me just short of catching up.

He leaned against the ball return, that infuriatingly charming smile still plastered on his face. "Looks like this one's mine."

I narrowed my eyes at him, trying not to let my disappointment show. "For now."

His grin widened. "Oh, don't worry, Layla. We've got plenty of games left. I'm sure you'll have your chance to catch up."

I rolled my eyes but couldn't help the small smile tugging at my lips. As much as I hated losing, there was something about this—about him—that made me look forward to the next game.

But it wasn't just the competition driving my feelings now. It was him—the way his hand casually brushed mine when he walked past, the way his voice dropped just enough to send a shiver down my spine, the way he looked at me like he was challenging me to do more than just bowl.

As the game ended and we started cleaning up, I found myself wondering where this was going. Because whatever this was between us, it was building into something more than just playful banter. It was desire, and the more I tried to ignore it, the more it consumed me.

Drake caught my gaze as we stood by the lanes, his eyes locking onto mine with an intensity that sent my heart racing. "You're a good bowler, Layla," he said softly, stepping closer, his voice smooth as silk. "But I have to say, I'm enjoying this more than I expected."

My breath hitched. "Me too."

His eyes darkened just slightly, his lips curving into a slow smile. "Good."

I swallowed hard, the tension between us thick enough to cut with a knife. And as I stood there, feeling the heat of his body just inches from mine.

CHAPTER FIVE

The third match started with a sense of familiarity, but the tension between us was anything but comfortable. Each game, each frame, was a dance of competitiveness and attraction, with neither of us willing to give an inch. And while our rivalry played out on the lanes, something else simmered just beneath the surface.

I lined up my shot, the weight of the ball steady in my hand. The focus I needed to win was there, but Drake wasn't making it easy. Every time I glanced at him, he was watching me with that same amused, cocky grin, his eyes trailing my movements with a heat that sent a rush of energy through me.

The ball left my fingers smoothly, curving just enough to catch the head pin perfectly. Strike. I allowed myself a small smile, glancing back to see

Drake shaking his head, though the smile on his face told me he wasn't upset.

"Nice shot," he said, stepping up for his turn. "But don't get too comfortable."

I leaned against the ball return, watching him. "I never do."

He lined up his shot with the same effortless confidence I'd come to expect. His muscles flexed as he released the ball, and like always, it was a strike. I resisted the urge to roll my eyes, but a part of me loved how evenly matched we were. It made everything more exciting.

Frame after frame, we exchanged strikes, spares, and the occasional teasing remark. But this game felt different—there was an edge to it, a push and pull that wasn't just about who would win. With each throw, each glance, I felt myself being pulled deeper into whatever this was between us.

Finally, the game came down to the last frame. We were tied, each of us needing a strike to pull ahead. I took a deep breath, lined up my shot, and sent the ball flying down the lane. It crashed into the pins with a satisfying crack. Strike.

Drake stepped up next, and I watched him with bated breath. His ball flew down the lane, perfect as always, and knocked every pin down.

"A tie," I said, crossing my arms and raising an eyebrow at him.

He grinned, walking back toward me. "Seems we're evenly matched."

"Seems that way," I replied, though my heart was pounding from more than just the game. The way he was looking at me—intense, playful, with something darker in his gaze—made my pulse quicken.

"How about we make things a little more interesting?" he asked, his voice dropping just enough to send a shiver down my spine.

I raised an eyebrow. "What do you have in mind?"

"Simple," he said, leaning casually against the ball return, his eyes never leaving mine. "Winner of the next match picks the drinks. Loser has to drink whatever the winner orders."

I bit my lip, considering. Part of me wanted to say no, to keep things purely competitive. But the way his eyes glinted with amusement, the way he seemed so sure of himself, made it hard to resist. And besides, there was no denying the spark between us.

"Alright," I said finally, crossing my arms. "You're on."

He grinned, that boyish, charming smile making my heart do a little flip. "Good. I like a woman who isn't afraid of a little challenge."

We started the next game with renewed energy,

and it wasn't just because of the bet. The chemistry between us had reached a boiling point.

But it wasn't just the game that had me on edge. It was the way he stood close to me. The way his hand would linger on my lower back just a second too long when he passed me. The way he would look at me, his eyes dark and full of something that made my breath catch in my throat.

I wasn't used to this—this feeling of being seen, of being wanted. Not after the divorce, not after years of feeling invisible in my marriage. But with Drake, it was different. He wasn't just looking at me like I was another competitor. He was looking at me like I was a woman—someone he desired, someone he wanted.

We were tied again, and I knew this last throw would determine the winner. But I wasn't just thinking about the drinks. I was thinking about what came after.

I stepped up, lined up my shot, and sent the ball down the lane. It hit perfectly, knocking all ten pins down. A strike. Three strikes in the last frame.

I turned back to Drake, my heart pounding. He was watching me, his gaze intense, a small smile playing at the corner of his lips.

"Nice," he said, his voice low. "But don't count me out yet."

He stepped up, his movements slow and deliberate, as if he knew exactly what he was doing to me.

His ball flew down the lane, knocking down all ten pins with ease. Three strikes in the last frame.

Another tie.

I shook my head, laughing softly. "You just won't let me win, will you?"

He stepped closer, so close I could feel the heat of his body. "Where's the fun in that?"

The air between us crackled with tension, the kind that made my skin tingle. I wasn't sure who leaned in first, but suddenly we were inches apart, our gazes locked.

"So," he said, his voice soft, his breath warm against my skin, "how about we call it a draw and both pick the drinks?"

I smiled, feeling more alive than I had in years. "Deal."

CHAPTER SIX

The low hum of conversation mixed with the clinking of glasses as I walked into the hotel bar. The dim lighting created an intimate atmosphere, and I could feel a slight tension in my chest, but not the bad kind. More like anticipation. I scanned the room, and there he was—Drake. He sat at the far end of the bar, his presence somehow commanding without even trying. When he saw me, he waved, his smile soft but enough to make my heart do a little flip.

I made my way over, trying to suppress the flutter of nerves. "Glad you could make it," he said as I took a seat beside him.

"I figured I could use a drink after today's game," I replied, settling onto the barstool. The air smelled of wood polish and something citrusy. It was comforting in a strange way.

Drake signaled the bartender. "What'll you have?"

"Maybe just a glass of chardonnay," I said, feeling like I needed something light.

He ordered a bourbon on the rocks and we sat there in a comfortable silence for a moment, the weight of the day starting to fade. Being around Drake, I didn't feel the pressure to perform, to pretend. I could just...be.

"So," Drake started, leaning his body slightly toward mine, "how long have you been into bowling? You've got quite the skill."

I let out a soft laugh. "Honestly? Bowling has been my escape. I've been playing for years but after the divorce, I needed something, anything, that wasn't tied to my old life. Bowling was the one thing that felt like mine."

He raised his glass to me. "I get that. Bowling's been my constant too. It's funny how we find solace in the strangest places."

I clinked my glass against his, feeling a bit more relaxed. "Yeah, funny." I took a sip, the crisp wine calming my nerves. "It hasn't been easy starting over, you know? Sometimes I feel like I'm still figuring it all out."

Drake's gaze softened. "Starting over is hard. But you're doing it. That's something to be proud of."

His words hit me harder than I expected. Maybe it was because I hadn't heard someone acknowledge it in a while—or maybe ever. "Thanks. Some days it doesn't feel like much."

"Trust me," he said, taking a sip of his drink. "You're doing more than most people do. You're still standing."

I smiled at that, but the warmth in my chest wasn't just from the wine. There was something about talking to Drake that made me feel…seen. Really seen. "What about you? You're here competing too. Is it just passion for the game, or…?"

He looked down at his glass for a moment, then back at me. "I love the sport, but it became more than that after I lost my wife."

I froze. I hadn't expected that. "I'm so sorry," I said quietly.

He nodded, but there was a calm acceptance in his eyes. "It's been years, but you never really get over it. You just…learn to keep moving. Bowling helped me with that. Gave me something to focus on when everything else felt too heavy."

I reached out, placing my hand on his for a moment. "I can't imagine what that must've been like."

He gave a small smile. "You do what you have to. You know how it is. You keep going because that's the only option."

I nodded, feeling the connection between us grow. "I guess I do."

It was strange—how easily I could talk to him,

how natural it felt to open up. I hadn't really talked about my divorce to anyone in such a real way. But with Drake, it didn't feel like I had to hold anything back.

"I haven't been kissed in a long time," I blurted out, surprising even myself. I felt my face heat up immediately.

Drake chuckled softly, but his eyes stayed on mine, warm and steady. "Yeah? Same here."

There was a pause, and I realized how close we were sitting. My heart picked up speed, and I felt a heat rise between us that I hadn't expected. Maybe it was the wine, or maybe it was just him, but I found myself leaning in slightly.

"I don't want to push," Drake said softly, his voice low, "but I'd be lying if I said I didn't feel something here."

I could barely breathe. "I feel it too."

Before I could second-guess myself, Drake leaned in, and suddenly his lips were on mine. The kiss started out soft, almost hesitant, but then it deepened, and I felt a surge of electricity run through me. It was like waking up a part of myself I hadn't realized had been asleep for so long.

I leaned into him, savoring the warmth of his mouth against mine, the way his hand gently cupped my face. It was like every nerve in my body was alive, buzzing with something new and thrilling. When we finally pulled away, my lips tingled, and I realized just how much I had missed this. Missed being kissed—really kissed.

Drake's forehead rested against mine for a moment, and I could hear the slight catch in his breath. "I hope that wasn't too forward."

I smiled, still trying to catch my own breath. "No, it was...perfect."

In that moment, I knew this wasn't just about bowling or passing the time. There was something real between us, something that felt right in a way I hadn't felt in years. And for the first time in a long time, I allowed myself to just be in it, to feel it, without any walls.

And damn, it felt good.

CHAPTER SEVEN

When we reach my suite, I hesitate outside the door, gripping the key card tightly. My heart races as I turn to look at Drake. He's standing close, his gaze steady, and something about the warmth in his eyes settles me. After a breath, I swipe the card and open the door, stepping inside with him behind me.

The door clicks shut, and for a moment, the silence between us feels charged, electrified. Drake takes my hand and pulls me close. This is the first time I've been with anyone since my ex, and it's like my entire body is trying to remember what this feels like—what this *could* feel like. But then his fingers caress my cheek, and his lips find mine, and I'm lost in him. I let go of my worries, surrendering to the way he draws me in.

His kisses start slow, tender, coaxing me into the

moment. His tongue runs along my lips and I part them Soon they become more intense, his lips parting against mine, drawing me deeper into him. He slips his hands under the hem of my shirt, sliding it up and over my head. I shiver as he tosses it aside, his hands roaming along my bare skin. I follow his lead, pulling his shirt off, letting my fingers glide over the hard lines of his chest. We're kissing like teenagers, caught up in the thrill, the vulnerability, the closeness.

Then his fingers slip to the clasp of my bra, unhooking it with a slow, practiced ease. He slides it from my shoulders, his gaze reverent as it falls away. His hands move to the button of my jeans, and I feel my breath catch as he eases them down, slipping them off with gentle hands. I do the same, tugging his jeans free until we're standing there, bare, exposed, vulnerable.

Drake leans in, his lips brushing over my neck, moving lower, trailing warmth and fire across my collarbone and down to my breasts. He takes one into his mouth, his tongue warm and insistent as he draws me closer. I gasp, feeling a coil of pleasure tightening low in my belly, and I'm unable to resist as I take his hand, leading him to the bed.

We lie down, and he presses a line of kisses along the back of my neck, igniting every nerve. Then he spreads my thighs, his touch finding my wet, aching center. He trails kisses down my stomach, stopping at the edge of my need, his breath hot against me. His tongue brushes my clit, and I can barely stifle a moan.

"You taste like honey and strawberries," he whispers, savoring me. He circles my clit in a rhythm that has me writhing beneath him, clinging to the sheets, begging him for more, breathless with need.

He pulls back, his gaze heated as he asks, "Are you sure?"

"Yes," I breathe, needing him in a way I hadn't known I could.

I close my eyes, and an image of my ex-husband flickers unbidden through my mind. I remember the first time we made love—young, in love, and full of the kind of hope that leaves no room for disappointment. Back then, the size of his cock hadn't mattered. When I told one of my girlfriends how big he was, they laughed. Full belly laugh. I thought the closeness, the feeling of connection, was enough to make up for everything else. I loved him, and I thought that was all we needed. But in the end, even that couldn't keep us together. He left me while sitting next to me, little by little. I remember that final conversation sinking into a numb silence, the space between us as vast as an ocean.

Now, here I am, the anticipation pulling me back into the present, feeling a flicker of nervousness and a thrill of excitement as I look at Drake. Everything about him is so different from what I'd known. I glance down, and I can't help but notice how he's thicker, longer, so much larger than my ex ever was. A part of me wonders how he'll fit.

And then, he's there, filling me in a way that feels whole, complete, and perfect. My breath catches as he presses deeper, stretching me in ways I hadn't imagined. His length fills every inch, pressing against parts of me that feel untouched, sending shocks of pleasure that radiate through my entire body. There's a rightness in the way he moves, in the way he makes me feel cherished and alive. I cling to him, feeling each thrust as he draws me into a rhythm that leaves me spiraling, senses over-whelmed, lost in the sensation of being truly, deeply wanted.

I moan, caught up in the pleasure of it, any coherent thought slipping away. He thrusts into me, his movements deep and sure, his body fitting against mine like he was made for me.

"I want to make you scream your pleasure," he says, his voice rough with desire. "You're going to come for me, Layla."

And with one last thrust, I do, my body shuddering around him, waves of ecstasy tearing through me, leaving me breathless and trembling. But he doesn't stop; his thrusts come harder, faster, and I feel the coil inside me tighten again, this time deeper, more intense.

"Don't stop," I gasp, my voice shaky, clinging to

him, my fingers digging into his shoulders as another climax builds within me. And then it explodes, pure pleasure surging through me like fireworks, the intensity filling me until I cry out, tears blurring my vision as euphoria washes over me, leaving me feeling whole.

For a long moment, we lie tangled together, catching our breath. I feel lighter, like something inside me has healed. I hadn't realized how much I needed this—how much I needed to feel truly desired, cherished. I'd spent years thinking that part of my life was over, that passion and intimacy were things I'd left behind. But here I am, feeling alive in a way I hadn't in years.

Drake pulls me close, his arms wrapped around me, and I rest my head against his chest, listening to his heartbeat.

I feel myself relaxing, warmth flooding my limbs as we lay tangled together, limbs intertwined, hearts slowly finding a shared rhythm. Drake's arms tighten around me, grounding me. His fingers trail along my shoulder, tracing lazy patterns that send little shivers through me. I close my eyes, letting the warmth of his embrace, the softness of his skin against mine, soothe something inside me that's felt unsettled for years.

The silence between us is full and comforting, allowing me to just be here, in this moment, feeling like I belong. There's no rush, no expectations—just two people sharing this space, and somehow, that's enough. I didn't realize how much I'd been carrying until it started to fall away, like weights lifting from my chest, one by one. I'm free in a way I hadn't thought possible.

Drake shifts beside me, propping himself up on an elbow, his gaze searching mine. "You good?" he asks, his voice soft.

I nod, a smile creeping onto my face as I meet his gaze. "Better than good," I whisper, brushing a hand through his hair. "Thank you...for everything." My words come out softer than I intended, and I hope he understands what I mean—that this wasn't just a night, but something much more.

He smiles, his hand coming to rest on my cheek, his thumb brushing gently along my jaw. "You deserve this, Layla—all of this."

I close my eyes, savoring the warmth in his voice, letting his words settle over me like a promise.

CHAPTER EIGHT

Waking up the next morning, I feel a warmth around me, and as my mind drifts back into focus, I realize I'm wrapped in Drake's arms. His body is pressed close behind me, spooning me, the slow rhythm of his breathing against my back both comforting and grounding. It's been so long since I've felt this... happy. I savor the sensation of his strong arms holding me, his chest firm against my back, his presence steady, real. There's a sense of contentment warming me from the inside, but then I notice another warmth—a heat pooling between my legs as I feel the unmistakable press of his erection against me.

Desire stirs, and without thinking, I roll over to face him, my hand instinctively reaching for him, feeling the warmth and hardness of him. Drake's eyes open, catching me with a lazy, smoldering smile. His lips find mine, and he kisses me deeply, slow and tender, his hand cupping the back of my head as though I might slip away. This time, there's no hurry, no sense of urgency—just the steady, consuming rhythm of his body joining mine. I feel every inch, every caress, every movement, fully. It's as though he's mapping each part of me, and I'm letting him. Each touch becomes a promise, each kiss a shared understanding that neither of us needs to speak.

Afterward, we make our way to the bathroom. I start the shower, feeling a little shy but excited, and he steps in with me, pulling me under the warm stream of water.

As the warm water cascades over us, I reach for the soap, working it into a lather before gliding my hands across Drake's shoulders, feeling the firm muscles under my fingertips.

"You're going to spoil me if you keep this up," he murmurs, his voice rough with sleep and a hint of laughter.

I grin, glancing up at him. "Think you deserve a little spoiling. Besides, when was the last time you actually took a relaxing morning?"

Drake chuckles, taking the soap from my hands and mimicking my movements, running his hands along my arms, sending little sparks along my skin. "Too long. Used to have a lot more lazy mornings, but now it's usually work, early practices, and driving back and forth."

"You have family nearby?" I ask, curious.

"No, not close by," he says, his hands moving to my shoulders, massaging gently. "Just me, really. It's been that way for a while. My wife passed years ago, and my folks are gone, too."

I pause, resting my hands on his chest, absorbing the quiet vulnerability in his words. "I'm sorry, Drake. That must have been hard."

"It was," he says softly, his gaze meeting mine. "But it taught me to appreciate the little things, you know? Even mornings like this—especially mornings like this."

I smile, tracing my fingers down his chest. "Mornings like this don't come around very often for me either."

"Not with two daughters, I imagine," he teases, his voice warm. "Tell me about them. They must be proud of you for being brave enough to start over."

"They can be a handful, but I couldn't be prouder. Both strong, smarter than I ever was at their age," I say, laughing. "They keep me on my toes and remind me there's still so much I want to do. Bowling became my escape, but now I want more than that."

Drake lifts a hand to my cheek, his thumb brushing against my skin. "And you deserve it,

Layla. You're taking your life back, on your own terms. It's…beautiful to watch."

His words wrap around me, filling a space I hadn't realized was empty. I touch his face, smiling. "And you? What else do you want out of life?"

He grins, tracing his hands down my back and pulling me closer. "Well, right now, I just want to keep making you smile. And maybe I'll throw in a strike or two today, for good measure."

I laugh, playfully nudging him. "You'll have to catch me first. I'm not planning on going easy on you."

"Oh, it's on," he says, pulling me into a slow, lingering kiss. The words fade, leaving only the gentle laughter, the warmth of his hands, and the quiet intimacy of the morning.

As we finish dressing, Drake reaches for my hand, pausing for a moment before we head to the door.

"Hey," he says, giving me that warm, steady gaze that feels like it's seeing straight through me. "Can I get your number?"

I laugh softly, realizing we hadn't even thought about it until now. "Of course." He hands me his phone, and I quickly typ my number and hand it back to him.

He smiles, saving it into his phone. "Perfect. I'll text you mine," he says, a spark of something warm and sure lighting his eyes. "This way, we don't have to rely on chance to see each other again."

I feel my face warm at his words, at the way he says them so simply, so casually, yet with an unmistakable certainty.

When we walk down to the lanes together, I can feel the shift within me, a new kind of confidence grounding each step. It's as if a part of me, dormant for so long, has been awakened. I feel like I'm stepping into myself in a way I never thought possible.

CHAPTER NINE

It's the final day of the tournament and there's an air of excitement and anticipation. As I step into the bowling alley, I scan the crowd, already feeling the familiar rush of competition. But today, it's different. Today, there's Drake. I spot him on the opposite side of the lanes, his eyes already searching for me.

When he finally catches my gaze, a slow smile spreads across his face, and I can feel the heat bloom in my chest. The energy between us has shifted, softer and closer, yet still charged with that undeniable spark. He heads over, hands in his pockets, looking so at ease it makes my stomach flip.

"Ready for one last match?" he asks, his eyes crinkling at the corners as he grins.

"Are you kidding? I was born ready," I say with a wink, and he chuckles, leaning in close enough that

I catch the faint scent of his cologne—a mix of cedar and something warm that sends shivers down my spine.

Our game is fierce and focused, but the rivalry has mellowed, replaced by a feeling of mutual respect and admiration. When he strikes, I clap and cheer; when I knock down a set, he's right there, flashing me a proud smile. The crowd's noise melts into the background, leaving only the steady rhythm of our friendly competition.

After a tense final round, I roll my last ball, watching as it spins down the lane, teetering on the edge of victory... and then, just barely, the last pin wobbles but stays upright.

"Almost!" I exclaim, laughing as I turn to Drake, who's grinning from ear to ear.

"Almost had me, Layla," he says, stepping closer. "You were amazing out there."

"I didn't win, though," I say, shrugging, though there's not a hint of disappointment inside me. I feel a new strength, a new sense of accomplishment that has nothing to do with winning.

"Maybe not," he says softly, reaching for my hand. "But I think we both know you've won something better."

The world around us seems to slow as he steps even closer, his hand warm in mine. I tip my face up to his, feeling that familiar thrill run through me. And then his lips meet mine, soft and tender, pulling me deeper into the moment. I wrap my arms around him, holding on as if he's the only solid thing in the room.

But then, just as quickly as it began, everything fades. The sounds of the alley, the smell of the oil-slicked lanes, the warmth of Drake's hand in mine—all of it slips away. I blink, finding myself lying on the cool black leather of the chaise lounge back in the Arcane Room.

I sit up slowly, heart pounding, still feeling the phantom press of his lips on mine. The Arcane Room came into focus, but part of me is still lingering on that last kiss, that sense of strength and joy I felt with him.

And as I look around, a small smile curls my lips. I didn't win the tournament, no. But I've walked away with something far more valuable—a sense of empowerment, a reminder of the strength I'd thought I'd lost, and the memory of a kiss that reminds me of the life and happiness still waiting for me.

CHAPTER TEN

I stood from the couch, still caught in the haze of what had just happened. Every touch, every kiss, every laugh with Drake had been so vivid, so real. I smoothed my shirt, the smile on my face refusing to fade. I couldn't help it—it had been incredible.

Ms. Vesper cleared her throat, her eyes twinkling like she already knew everything I was thinking. "Someone seems to be all smiles."

I let out a soft chuckle, still in awe of the experience. "It was amazing... I had no idea this was even a thing. It's just... so cool. How does this all work?"

Ms. Vesper smiled, that mysterious, knowing look never leaving her face. "The cards always know, dear. You drew the Seven of Wands, remember?"

I nodded, recalling the card I'd pulled at the start

of all this. "Yeah, the Seven of Wands... but what does that mean?"

She stepped a little closer, her voice lowering as though sharing a secret. "The Seven of Wands is about standing your ground, fighting through obstacles. But more than that, it's about finding your inner strength, about realizing what you're truly capable of. For you, Layla, this wasn't just about bowling, was it?"

Her words struck me in a way I didn't expect. "No... no, it wasn't," I admitted, feeling a strange mix of gratitude and understanding wash over me.

"That's the magic of the Arcane Room," she continued, her voice soft. "The cards reflect what you need. The experience? It helps you find it."

I could only nod, feeling a deep sense of peace and empowerment as I left the Arcane Room. After buying a couple of candles that caught my eye—one for protection, the other for peace—I headed home. I wasn't in any rush. The day had already been full, and I wanted to savor the feeling of being... well, content. Truly content.

Once I got home and settled onto my couch, I realized I hadn't checked my phone all day. I grabbed it from my bag and unlocked the screen. A single text message was waiting for me—from an unknown number.

I had a wonderful time with you today. Would love to FaceTime later, if you're up for it?

My heart skipped a beat. Could it be him? My mind raced, but before I could respond, another message popped up.

Oh, it's me—Drake Harper. Just wanted to make sure you knew it wasn't some random guy texting you, haha.

I let out a small laugh, relief and excitement bubbling up inside me. Drake. He was real. It wasn't just some fantasy cooked up by the Arcane Room. I quickly typed back.

I had an amazing time too! I'd love to FaceTime later.

I hit send, feeling my fingers tremble just a little. Before I could even fully process the butterflies in my stomach, another text came through.

By the way, where are you from?

Without thinking too hard about it, I typed back.

Coral Cove.

A few seconds passed, and then his response popped up on the screen.

No way. Are you lying?

I grinned, shaking my head.

Why would I lie about that?

I live in Coral Cove too. This is crazy... We were so close this whole time!

I laughed out loud at the sheer coincidence of it all—or was it even a coincidence? Maybe there was more magic at play than I thought.

Looks like we're neighbors.

I texted back, adding a little smiley face for good measure.

How about we meet for dinner tomorrow? Golden Chopsticks? 7 pm?

The world seemed to open up in that moment, as if the magic of the Arcane Room had spilled into real life, weaving Drake into my story in a way I never saw coming.

It's a date. See you tomorrow, Drake.

Hitting send, I leaned back against the couch, a smile still playing on my lips. The excitement buzzing through me felt like a promise of something new. Something real. I wasn't just surviving anymore—no, I was thriving. Tomorrow, I'd take another step toward whatever was next.

With a deep, contented sigh, I closed my eyes, letting the warmth of anticipation fill me. This was just the beginning. And I was ready.

THANK you for reading Seven of Wands. If you enjoyed this book, please check out some of my other titles, including **The Perfect Lover Spell.**

JESSA: The love spell I cast was supposed to be a joke. But now a Scotsman from 2014 is in my living room. We must reverse the magic before he's stuck here forever. But I'm falling for the perfect lover I never expected.

BRYCE: One moment, I'm in Scotland; the next, I'm in Jessa's world. This love spell has bound us together. But can we break it before I lose my heart to the enchanting woman who summoned me?

A LOVE SPELL with unexpected results.

Jessa's love life has been a series of disasters, from awkward dates to toxic relationships. Tired of swiping left and right, she's ready to give up on finding her perfect match. But when her best friend pushes her to try something different—a love spell from the mysterious Spellbound Stories bookstore— Jessa decides to take a chance on magic. Little does she know that casting The Perfect Lover Spell will bring more than she bargained for.

Enter Bryce MacGregor, a handsome and rugged Scotsman who literally appears out of nowhere... from ten years in the past. Struggling to make sense of his sudden time travel, Bryce must navigate modern-day Coral Cove while Jessa tries to reverse the spell. But as they spend more time together, the line between magic and reality blurs, and sparks begin to fly.

Can Jessa and Bryce find a way to break the spell

without breaking their hearts? Or has fate—and a little magic—brought them together for a reason?

The Perfect Lover Spell is a steamy, time-travel romance that blends humor, magic, and a sizzling connection that defies time itself. Perfect for fans of magical realism and heartwarming love stories.

SIGN up for my newsletter and get a free book today! https://mailchi.mp/158597581671/jax-wilder

ALSO BY JAX WILDER

Coral Cove Series

Sleighed by Love

Harvesting Love

Dawning Desire

Knead You Now

Love Rewound

Perfect Lover Spell

Haunted by Her

Red, White, and Ravished

Tarot Fantasies Series

The Devil's Temptations

Strength of the Beast

Hanged Passions

Six of Cups

Death's Embrace

Queen of Pentacles

Seven of Pentacles

Ace of Wands

Three of Swords

Lovers In The Veil

<u>Two of Swords</u>

Coastal Cupid Series

HeartBound Souls

Fae Ring Series

Alice and Her Mad Hatters

Stand Alone Titles

Pride and Prejudice and Witches

Additional Books by

Rainbow Quartz Publishing

Lorelai Hamilton

Encyclopedia of Divination

Encyclopedia of Cryptids

Encyclopedia of Faeries

Tarot Tales and Magic Spells

Teenage Tarot

Arcane In Verse

The Eclectic Witch's Grimoire

Teenage Witch's Grimoire

Find Your Bliss

Tarot Reflection Journal

Tarot Refection Journal Coloring The Tarot

Dream Journal

Miranda Levi

From A Youth A Fountain Did Flow

The Sea Withdrew

A Tear In Time

Mo(ther) Na(ture)

In Orion's Hands

Jackson Anhalt

From The 911 Files

Isla Watts

A Fairy Bad Day

Surprise! You're a Vampire

Gorgeous, Gorgeous, Gorgons

Mork The Handsome Orc

Adopted By Werewolves

Bite Me If You Can

That's The Spirit!

Rose Dawson's Book Journals

My Time With The Fairies

Enchanted Escapades

Enchanted Escapades

Dewey Decimal Diaries

Siren's Songbook

Pride and Prejudice

Bibliophile's Bounty

Book of Books Journal

Pages & Passages Reading Journal

Bookworm's Companion Reading Journal & Tracker